Disguised Arrogance
Revealed Demise

by

Brigette A. Ways

PublishAmerica
Baltimore

© 2007 by Brigette A. Ways.
All rights reserved. No part of this book may be reproduced, stored in a retrieval system or transmitted in any form or by any means without the prior written permission of the publishers, except by a reviewer who may quote brief passages in a review to be printed in a newspaper, magazine or journal.

First printing

All characters appearing in this work are fictitious. Any resemblance to real persons, living or dead, is purely coincidental.

ISBN: 1-4241-7646-8
PUBLISHED BY PUBLISHAMERICA, LLLP
www.publishamerica.com
Baltimore

Printed in the United States of America

I dedicate this book to my mother, Maxine L. Stowers. A woman who became the loudest cheerleader in thanking God for what he has done in my life. She believed in his word that stated that my gift would make room for me.

Acknowledgment

I want to acknowledge first, the Lord and Savior of my life, my daughters, Erica and Brettaney, my six sisters, Sharon, Crystal, Toni, Sheila, Leslie and Stacy, and my brother, Nathan and my agent, Antriece Hart.

CONTENTS

Chapter One: Boxed In   9

Chapter Two: Pained Toward Action   14

Chapter Three: A Stranger Calls   21

Chapter Four: Exposed Truths   26

Chapter Five: Rode   31

Chapter Six: Inherited Damnation   36

Chapter Seven: Bewildered   45

Chapter Eight: Freedom Rings   50

Chapter Nine: Old Acquaintances, New Choices   54

Chapter Ten: Betrayal of a Perpetrator   59

Chapter Eleven: Employed with a Cost   62

Chapter Twelve: Through the Eyes of a Conscience   67

Chapter One
Boxed In

Sheniece was twelve years old at the time. She was the only child of Marisa, a divorced mother who had earned a degree in fashion designing. Marisa never utilized her degree because she married and became pregnant shortly afterwards. However, her husband appeared to lose interest in her after the birth of her daughter. He began staying away from home night after night. Marisa tried everything she could to lose weight. Her efforts included going to the gym five days a week for four hours a class. She changed her hairstyle and began wearing revealing clothes. It did not work. He left after a year of being married.

Marisa's feeling of hurt and abandonment turned into bitterness. She concealed her torment from Sheniece until she was ten years old and had begun to take on the features of her father. Marisa's interaction with her daughter symbolized the relationship between a tyrant and the people he oppressed. This was the only representation of control in Marisa's life, the control she had over this vulnerable little girl. She held nothing back in her strict rearing, motivated by the pain and anger seething inside her heart. Sheniece had become the recipient of her own mother's inability to move from her past.

Sheniece was given a strict regiment that she had to follow to the letter. She had to be out of bed by 6:00 a.m. Her alarm clock could only ring twice. If it rang more than the two times, Sheniece was greeted with a glass of ice water being poured on her. Her body would cringe, with chill bumps rising up on her skin.

"Why did you do that, Mom?" Sheniece would scream.

Marisa would calmly respond by saying, "You have to be up before the sun rises."

"Why?" Sheniece asked in disbelief.

This question seemed to ignite a feeling of power in Marisa. It was as if she had encountered a moment of relief from her own inner torment and, with a sense of arrogance, she would meticulously state, "Because I say so."

This form of dysfunctional parenting continued well into Sheniece's teenage years. Her mother was still unable to break the emotional choke hold ,that suffocated her ability to be rational. As a result, Sheniece lived in an ongoing world of intimidation and fear.

However, in spite of her emotional prison, physically she had grown into a beautiful young girl. She stood out amongst the girls and was noticed by all of the boys. But, her anti-social behavior superseded her looks. She attempted to explain her behavior by telling them that she didn't have time to socialize because of her studies, when, in truth, she was dying to fit in with her peers. They finally invited her to study with them at the library. Sheniece was assured that this request would be granted since it was school related.

"Mom, can I meet with some of my friends to study together at the library," she asked. She was positive that her mother would loosen her grip for this good cause.

Again, Marisa became ignited with a sense of sheer empowerment. She turned to Sheniece without any presence of emotion and said no.

Astounded by this response, Sheniece, almost in tears, asked, "Why not?"

Marisa had gained another moment to demonstrate her control, and, without hesitation, said, "Because I say so."

This picture was played out over and over again in the life of this mother and daughter.

Sheniece was now sixteen years of age and had developed into an antisocial and submissive young woman. Her disposition was further complicated by the fact that she was a pretty girl and often approached by many of the guys. This admiration was in conflict with the life she had come to know. *What were they seeing that her mother did not?* She wondered. This unanswered question dominated her every waking moment. Why had her mother become the sore that would not heal in her life?

One day she attempted to get this questioned answered by the perpetrator herself. She had to find a rational reason for her mother's refusal to acknowledge her existence. This action would serve as the fuel needed to launch Marisa's rage toward her.

"Mom, why don't you ever let me go out with my friends?" she asked. She went on to plead her case. "I have never been to the mall, the movies, or even to visit them at their homes," she asked in a sheepish manner. Sheniece firmly stated that everyone thought that she was strange.

Marisa, shocked by Sheniece's somewhat bold behavior, poured out her rage with a vengeance. "Who do you think that you're talking to? I am your mother! The one who kept you, even when your father did not want you? I am the one who gave up on my dreams in order to have a baby by a man who was not true! You dare to question me? You're just selfish and ungrateful."

Sheniece yells out, "It is not like that! I just wanted to know, why do you always say no to every request that I make to you?" Sheniece pleaded.

Marisa, ignoring her daughter's genuine concern, slowly turned and indignantly said, "Because I say so, and I do not owe you any explanations."

This explosive dialogue was the spark that caused Sheniece to spiral on a destructive path, a path that would dictate the encounters she would experience in her future. Sheniece had come to accept that she was the dump site for her mother's misery. Therefore, she relinquished any hope of having a relationship with her. But, she yearned to have closeness and began seeking comfort from the boys who showed her attention. Yes, the boys who told her she had it going on. She forced herself to crawl out of the shell that had been thrust upon her. Sheniece had become every boys fantasy and every girls envy. She was in the in crowd. She began to skip school, hanging out at all of the forbidden places. She went to the movies, to the malls and hung out at the homes of her friends. Sheniece was no longer the odd girl at school. She would also embrace the habits of her new friends. She began smoking cigarettes, drinking and smoking marijuana. But, she also carried the burden of living a dual life and hiding it from the person who created it.

Marisa had finally gotten a job in designing and was never home. As a result, she did not observe the changes occurring in Sheniece's personality. She was confident that her tyrant style of child rearing would keep her daughter from straying. Marisa's security in her tactics would soon crumble.

In the meantime, Sheniece had become mesmerized by an older man. This twenty-five-year-old man had fed into the emptiness of her soul. He told her that she was the epitome of what a woman should be. He held her hand in public, proving to her that she was special to him. He gave her flowers and took her to the movies. He would be the one who would rescue her from a life that had her boxed in. There would not be any more loneliness or confusion.

Sheniece was becoming abrasive in the choices she made. The love she had for him conquered any fears she had regarding her mother. She was always at his house. Sheniece had become his woman in every aspect. She had lost her innocence to the love of her life. She resigned to living with him forever. She would not return to the site of her mother's living hell.

But his plans for the future did not include her. Sheniece succumbed to a pain that she had never known before. He told her of his thoughts. She had been accustomed to the effects of a mother's rejection, but this pierced her heart much deeper than anything her mother had said or done to her. She tried desperately to hold back her tears, concealing the true hurricane that was taking over inside her. He explained that he had plans that would not allow him to be in a committed relationship. He then encouraged her to go home and back to school.

Sheniece was frozen with silence, unable to respond to the perpetrator of her new pain. She got up slowly, hoping not to uncover the weakness she felt in her legs. He empathetically questioned her understanding of his words. Without looking at him, she conceded to the breakup by nodding her head and walked out the door.

She returned to the nest that awaited her with chains. At least its hold on her was never disguised as being nothing other than contempt.

Chapter Two
Pained Toward Action

Sheniece had returned to what she had become used to. It was however, to her pleasure that her mother had become too busy to focus on her. She had no idea that her daughter was no longer naive to the outside world and although she attempted to revert back to the obedient and docile child that she had been raised to become, this would be difficult. She had experienced a touch of womanhood which could not be converted back to an innocent girl. The evidence of this truth made its presence known. Sheniece's body had begun a metamorphosis. Her hips had spread, her breasts enlarged and her period ceased. She was pregnant. Nothing else that had taken place before this could measure up to the earthquake about to take place. How could she tell her mother? What would be the backlash of her actions? Would the mother who had already shown contempt for her deepen her rejection? What about him? Would he recant the words that he had spoken three months earlier? Or would she relive the pain inflicted on her heart?

Her fear began to turn to anguish. Her eyes swelled up with the tears, wanting to be released. The freedom of their existence was created because there was no one to judge their presence and cry she did. Sheniece knew that the time to tell her mother was fast approaching. *If my mother had been attentive to me, she would know that I was pregnant*, she thought to herself. *She would be the one having to think of a way to ask me*, she pondered. But, the worry was all on her. Sheniece also knew that it would be a possibility that Marisa would put her out.

So, Sheniece began planning ahead for what she would do. Her life was about to change. She would have to get a job. She decided to find a job and get her GED. This had to be done before exposing her secret. She would not tell the father about the baby, for fear of him denying her child. She refused to turn into a bitter woman. Her child would not become the victim of her past mistakes. She would be a good mother.

Sheniece got a job as a restaurant server, then enrolled in a GED program. She wore large clothes and was away from home as much as her mother was. She held off on the inevitable conversation until her pregnancy could no longer be concealed. She had saved up enough money to get her own place if she was kicked out of her mother's house. After all, how could she love her grandchild when she was unable to love the one birthed from her own womb? She had also successfully obtained her GED certificate. She was prepared for the raft of emotional daggers that would be targeted at her.

Sheniece decided to divulge her secret on a day that Marisa had stayed home from work sick in bed. She would be too weak to penetrate her pain with much force.

"Mom! There is something that I have to tell you." Sheniece said with a sly smirk and slight meekness.

Marisa's facial expression told her that she did not want to be bothered, but she had no choice. She would have to listen.

Then, without hesitation, Sheniece said, "I am pregnant."

Marisa slowly sat up from her lying position. "You are what!" she said with genuine shock.

Sheniece began blurting out her plans, as if it would alleviate her mother's fury. "I got my GED, I got a job, I have money saved up and I am going to get my own place." She waited for her mother to say, I'm disappointed but we can work it out. Those words were never to come.

"Get out of my house!" Marisa screamed. She raged on. "You're crazy if you think that I am going to raise your child. Not on your life. I gave up so much for you and your father and I will not do it again!"

Sheniece felt a burning flame rising up in her and before she knew it she lashed back at her mother. "What did you give up for me? Tell me! You gave up your life for a man who did not want you and all you have done is beat me up because of it. I am sick of being the recipient of your pain. If you want me to leave, I will. But, you need to direct your anger at the one who hurt you and not at the product of the love you had for him. I am not your enemy." She had finally emptied out the contents of the emotional toxins that were eating her alive.

Marisa stared up at her daughter and, with the screech of a wounded animal who had just been defeated, weakly said, "Get out of my house."

At that moment it was if Sheniece had matured by ten years. She stared back at her mother and, with the pride of wining general, she said with great authority, "I will pack my things and leave at the end of the week."

Marisa, stunned and frozen in place, could only retreat in silence, for she had lost control over the only one who was unable to strike back at her.

Sheniece was on the road of adulthood. She found a one bedroom apartment and began her journey as a soon to be single mother.

Most young mothers would exhibit some fear over this new experience, but, for Sheniece, it was the beginning of her freedom. There would be no more painstaking denials of her request to just live. She would be the ruler of her palace. She continued working until she was able to buy a bed, a sofa, table and chairs. She had taken her television, DVD player, bedding and her famous clock from her bedroom in her mother's house. Her boss had given her dishes and other kitchen utensils. She was now ready to explore the area around her palace and, to her surprise, she lived in a building where some of her peers lived. Everything was working out as she had hoped. Sheniece was ready to celebrate her independence.

She invited two classmates to celebrate with her. She placed a bowl of chips on a small table. Feeling a sense of exhilaration, she stepped back to marvel at her accomplishment. Her moment of euphoria was interrupted by a knock at her door. It was her "friends" Daryl and Danay.

Danay was short and round, with an unusual confident demeanor. This confidence was created by her ability to accept her own shortcomings, which prevented her from being affected by the insults of others. She had a way of setting the tone for how a conversation would take place.

Daryl was a tall, slim and loud man, and was considered to be the class clown. He could take the most serious discussion and turn it in to a joke.

Sheniece invited them in, offering them some chips, then admitting to only having water for them to drink.

Daryl, with his usual sense of humor, eased Sheniece's concern. "Girl, that's quite alright. I know what it means to be poor. We were so poor that my mother would boil water, add salt and call it clear soup. I did not know that it was not really soup until I went to the dentist with a toothache. He told me to go home and gargle with salt and water. I looked at him and said, 'With soup?' Child, that dentist still laughs when I go to his office."

Danay was overcome with laughter at Daryl's story. "Boy, you are crazy! she hollered.

"I declare that it's true." Daryl continued his story by stating that when he returned home, he asked his mother how come she made him believe that plain water and salt was soup? He said that she answered by asking him a question. "If I had told you that we were having salt and water for dinner, would you have come running to eat?" Daryl admittedly stated, that was the end of that conversation.

The topic took Sheniece back to her own childhood. "At least you could ask a question. Living in my house was like being in the Army. Everything was because my mother said so. I would ask if I could go to the mall. She would say no. I would ask why? Her response was always because she said so. I did not mind that she said no. It just bothered me because it seemed as if she just liked being in control." Sheniece, rubbing her stomach, declared that she was going to name her unborn child Sayso. It would serve as a reminder never to treat her son like she was treated.

Danay did not believe that Sheniece was serious.

Daryl jokingly said, "Whatever you say so, will be so."

Danay joined in by laughing. Sheniece realized that Danay and Daryl did not understand the sincerity of her heart. Irritated, she wished for the visit to end and so she let out a huge yawn.

Danay caught on immediately. "Well, I got to go."

Daryl followed her lead and got up to leave too.

"I'll see you guys later," Sheniece said, as she quickly closed the door, just in case they changed their minds about leaving. She returned to admiring the solace of her palace, when a sudden flow of water came streaming down her legs. This is followed by increasingly strong pain. She called her doctor, who then informed her that she was in labor and should go immediately to the hospital.

Sheniece arrived at the hospital by ambulance. She was put into a birthing room hooked up to a monitor and left alone to hear the sound of her baby's heart beat. She looked outside her room and noticed the fathers and grandmothers there to see the other babies. There was no one there for her. She thought about calling Marisa, but could not chance being rejected.

She had no clue about the father's whereabouts, and even if she did she would not call him. He had already shown her that he did not want to have anything do with her. She would do this alone. She would soon have a baby that she could love and who would love her back. No more rejection.

Sheniece did it. She gave birth to a healthy baby boy. Sayso Dajon. She loved Sayso with all of her heart and was determined to become a good mother. She had no support, but it did not matter. She would do all that it took to take care of him, especially his emotional needs. She fed him, bathed him, read to him, and hugged and kissed him constantly.

She never let him out of her sight. Not until he was six years of age, when at the coaxing of Daryl and Danay she did just that. They asked her to join them at a club. She refused, but Daryl would not take no for an answer. He gave her a vivid description of how her life was going to be if she did not get out of the house. He told her that she would end up a lonely old woman. He added a bleaker picture when he told her that she would end up despising Sayso for giving up her life for him. These were the words which would motivate her to make a choice, which would change the path of both their lives

"Okay, I'll go." She did not want to develop the characteristics of her own mother. "You guys go ahead. I'll meet you there."

She had to get a babysitter. But the only person that she could ask was Marisa. Maybe she had changed her heartless ways. Maybe she had gotten over the pain of being dumped and could now be a grandmother to Sayso. Sheniece found the courage to call her mother. After all, it had been six years. A grandmother should want to have a relationship with her only grandchild.

"Hello," Marisa answered.

Sheniece immediately heard the same old voice of a woman scorned. She thought about hanging up, but felt compelled to respond to her mother's second hello. "Hello, Mom," Sheniece said with great hesitation, then there was complete silence.

"Mom!" she said, wanting to believe that she was not heard the first time, although she knew that this was not the case.

Marisa answered without any enthusiasm. "Hello, Sheniece. What took you so long to call?"

"I wanted to, but I did not know if you were still mad at me for getting pregnant," Sheniece explained in an apologetic tone.

"Well, what made you decide to call now?" apparently not moved by her daughter's apology.

"I was thinking that I might bring your grandson to see you."

How long do you plan to stay?" Marisa asked, as if they would be in her way.

"I actually wanted to know if you could keep him overnight? My friends asked me to go out tonight, but I do not have a babysitter."

There was a short pause, then Marisa said, "And you still don't." She went on to say that she had given all that she was going to give.

Taken back by her mother's absolute disconnection, Sheniece fired back with the same vengeance. "This is your only grandchild and you have never laid your eyes on him! Why can't you watch him?"

Marisa ended the conversation as cold as she had begun it. "Because I say so," she responded.

There they were again. The words that had been used to bind her for sixteen years. But this time, their sting was unable to penetrate or hold her hostage. "You're so self-centered that you did not even ask what his name is. Well, his name is Sayso. I named him that as a reminder not to treat him the way you treated me," Sheniece admitted. Finally, with the pride of a winning politician, she confronted her strong hold. "It's your loss, and one day when you're a lonely old woman, don't come looking for me or my son." Click. The strong hold had been cast down.

Chapter Three
A Stranger Calls

Without realizing it, Marisa's arrogance would continue to attach itself to Sheniece, for the decisions she made were motivated by their dysfunctional relationship.

I don't need her, she thought, and with that revelation she decided to leave Sayso home alone. She put him to sleep, turned out the light and locked the door behind her. As she was walking, she felt exhilarated by her freedom and, at the same time, guilty about leaving her child. She was met by a large man going into the building. She spoke and then asked if he lived in the complex. He said yes, then disappeared behind the door.

Knowing that this large man lived in the building gave her a reprieve from her guilt. Surely, this strong man would be the watchman over her palace.

Sheniece got to the club. She immediately spotted Daryl and Danay. "Hey, you didn't think that I would make it, huh?"

"Alright, super mama," Daryl said as he acknowledged her presence.

Sheniece was quickly pulled on to the dance floor by a handsome man. She danced with the freedom of a bird, free at last from her past and her present circumstances. Then, as fast as she had proclaimed her freedom, she was again bound by what her eyes saw.

There was the love of her life with his arm wrapped around another woman. The woman was beautiful, and on her finger was a gorgeous wedding ring. *What happened to his plans that did not include him being in a committed relationship?* The memory of the day that he rejected her re-surfaced. This was followed by a feeling of weakness and nausea. *How could he take her heart and then reject her like a piece of dirt? And what about the child she conceived with him? How could he act as if she never existed?* Her brain became cluttered with why, and then he turned in her direction. His eyes meet with hers. She did not know if she should run or ignore him.

He came walking toward her, bringing his wife with him. She braced herself for the encounter. There was no avoiding it.

"Hi, Sheniece. It's good to see you," he said as if they never had a past.

I dare that he act as if I'm just some kid on the block! she wanted to scream, but the only word that came out was, "Hello."

He then introduced his wife with the pride of a committed husband, then questioned her about what she had been doing.

She glanced at him with utter disgust. At that point, she knew that the secret of her son's birth would be the leverage that would break up his perfect life. She would choose when and where to drop the bomb. She would make him pay for the abandonment of her and her son. But, she would not allow him to turn her into a bitter and lonely woman like her mother She smiled and kindly stated that she's been taking care of her responsibilities. She wished him good luck, and he and his wife walked off into the dim lights.

Sheniece continued dancing and drinking all night long. She had gotten the attention of several men and she loved it. She celebrated her victory, for she had shown that she was stronger than her mother.

DISGUISED ARROGANCE

The evening had come and gone and it was now four in the morning. Her friends had gone hours ago. Sheniece was escorted by a man that she met at the club. She thanked him before shutting her door. Sayso was still sleeping. She prided herself on training him to sleep throughout the night.

She got in the bed, but was unable to fall asleep. She was absorbing the thrill of the evening and planned to go out again.

She had become addicted to the night life and went out on a regular basis. She developed a ritual of putting Sayso to bed, turning out the lights and locking her door.

But, on one particular night, a man invited her out earlier than usual. He insisted that she get ready immediately. Sheniece was forced to change her routine. Sayso was awake. She fed him, turned on the television, sat him on the couch and kissed him before telling him that she had to go out for a little bit. Her inpatient friend was outside blowing his car horn. She ran out the door, and in her haste, she left the door unlocked and slightly open.

Sayso sat obediently as he was told, confident that his mother would return.

Boomer, the large man that Sheniece had seen earlier, noticed that her door was open and observed Sayso sitting on the couch. He peeked in. "You alright, little man?" Boomer asked.

Startled by the intrusion, Sayso sheepishly said, "Un huh. My mommy will be back later."

Boomer smirked with the pride of a predator that had just captured his prey. He lied by telling Sayso that Sheniece had asked him to babysit for her.

Surprised, Sayso responded, "She did?"

"Yep," Boomer slyly admitted as he picked up the innocent little boy. "Are you hungry?" this predator asked.

"Yes sir," Sayso said with the politeness of a child being grateful for the kindness of an adult.

Boomer took Sayso to his apartment.

Sayso was immediately mesmerized by all of the toys he saw.

"Wow! You have a lot of toys. Do you got a little boy like me?" he asked with the intuitiveness that kids have.

"My kids are big," Boomer said.

"Then why do you have toys?"

"I keep them for the kids that don't have any." Boomer continued his subtle manipulation. "But, they have to play in my apartment, so that they are not stolen."

He then allowed Sayso to eat as much as he could and play until he was exhausted. When he fell asleep from exhaustion, Boomer put him in his bed where he proceeds to rob this six year old of his innocence.

Sheniece's love of her life had become the victim of her innocent negligence and immorality of a neighbor.

Boomer returned him home, sat him on the couch, hugged him and then told Sayso that he loved him and his mother. Before leaving, he told Sayso not to open the door. He left, shutting and locking the door behind him.

The darkness had turned into daylight and the birds were chirping. The door opened. Sheniece came in, surprised that her son was still awake.

"Oh, baby! I'm so sorry for getting back so late. Are you alright?" she asked, oblivious to Sayso's strange disposition.

He never answered her with words. He just sat and starred intently into her eyes. And then there was a knock at the door. It was Boomer.

"Hey, neighbor! I noticed that you had a little boy and wanted to give him this bike. My nephew outgrew it."

Filled with gratitude, Sheniece directed Sayso to say thank you to Boomer. But Sayso never opened his mouth. He just continued staring at his mother.

"What's wrong with you, son? Say thank you!" Apologizing for Sayso, she assured Boomer that she had raised her son better.

Seizing the opportunity to play the caring neighbor, he dismissed his victim's disregard and even offered to take him out bike riding.

DISGUISED ARROGANCE

Believing that this man's actions were honorable, she took him up on his offer.

Sheniece continued to entrust Sayso with Boomer and the abuse went on for seven years. He had become entrapped in a world of abuse, with no one to defend for him. The only person that could protect him was blinded by the kindness of a sly perpetrator.

As Sayso grew older; he began to experience feelings of guilt and shame. This led him to find solace in the seduction of the streets. He began using and selling drugs, fighting, stealing and using young girls. The streets had become the bandage covering his pain. People either admired or feared him.

A young boy and his mother moved into the complex. Sayso became immediately concerned about this boy becoming another victim of Boomer's. He was determined to keep that from happening. He saw the boy in front of the building one day. Sayso took the opportunity to talk with the young child.

"Hey, man, what's your name?"

"DaQuan," the boy answered.

"You just move in?" hoping to engage DaQuan into a conversation.

"Yep, me and my momma. Do you live here too?"

"All my life," Sayso divulged. "and I know everybody who lives here. So if a man name Boomer ever invites you into his house, don't go! Don't take money, toys or anything else from him."

"Why? Did he kill somebody?" DaQuan asked.

"Something like that," Sayso responded, careful not to display his own inner turmoil.

"DaQuan!"

"I gotta go. My mother is calling me." DaQuan got up to leave.

"Don't forget what I told you," Sayso urged the young boy. He felt good about his deed. He had prevented Boomer from destroying the life of another child. He considered himself to be DaQuan's guardian angel. It was too late for him, but not for another child moving into the building.

However, his feeling of heroism was interrupted when he received a call. His heart sank to the deepest darkest area of his soul because the voice on the other end of the receiver belonged to the murderer of his spirit.

Sayso was enraged at the arrogance of this thief. He ran into the building with every plan of killing this perpetrator. Sayso pounded on Boomer's door, causing a woman to look out her door. His anger blinded him to her presence.

"Come in, the door is open," the friendly voice said on the other side of the door.

These words increased his anger for Boomer, for that's how this man was able to destroy his life. Through an opened door Sayso was relentless in unleashing his fury.

"Man, it stops today! You have called me for the last time!"

Appearing not to understand Sayso's anger toward him, Boomer said, "I gave you everything and this is how you repay me!" Boomer responded.

"Pay you!" Sayso refuted. "You stole my childhood, my innocence. Man, you stole my spirit," almost in tears, "and I can never get those things back."

Boomer jumped up from his seat and declared, "I gave you my affection when your own father wasn't around! But be gone. I'm done with you."

Lunging at Boomer and grabbing his neck, Sayso said, "Be gone! I wish that I could rid my brain of your face. But you see, I can't because the smell of your foul breath forever permeates my nostrils!" Sayso lets go, pulls out a gun and said, "I could kill you, but I will have my day. You're not worth hanging myself out to dry." He then runs down the steps and out the building.

Ms. Real, the neighbor, was sickened by what she heard and ran to inform Sheniece.

Chapter Four
Exposed Truths

Ms. Real struggled with everything in her to make it to Sheniece's apartment. Her rage preceded her legs and her compassion for Sayso brought tears to her eyes. She pounded on the door, anxious to expose the truth.

Sheniece is annoyed by the pounding and responded with an abrupt, "Come in!"

Ms. Real stepped in and immediately began telling her story. "Miss, I overheard your son and that Boomer man arguing, and from the sound of things he had been molesting your boy for a long time," she said.

Sheniece looked at her as if she had spoken in another language. "You are out of your mind, lady!" She went on to say that Boomer had been the only man that looked out for them and never once had he ever looked at Sayso wrong.

"Oh no, baby, he had you fooled," Ms. Real replied with frustration. She paused, then asked, "Honey, have you ever seen his silent tears? Believe me, they were there," she declared.

Sheniece was in complete denial that this thing had happened and threw Ms. Real out of her apartment. Sheniece called out for

Sayso, positive that he would make a liar of the woman who brought her such bad tidings.

He didn't answer. She decided to have Boomer clear up the misunderstanding. She knocked on his door.

Boomer, thinking that Sayso had returned, yelled out, "What do you want? I said all that I have to say to you!"

Sheniece was troubled by his arrogant demeanor. She questioned him without hesitation. "It's me and I want to know what you did to my son?"

Boomer, surprised by her presence, realized that his back was against the wall. "What did he tell you I did?" throwing the question back at her.

Astounded by his behavior, she knew that it was all true. He had indeed molested her son. She was overcome with a feeling of sickness and hysteria. "You did it!" She plunged at him as he sat at his dinner table. "I trusted you with my baby and you put him in your bed!"

Boomer grabbed her arms before she could strike him and than, with the same expression of an cold corpse, said, "No, you put him in my bed by leaving him night after night."

Sheniece was mortified. "I didn't leave him for you to molest, you sick creep. I thought that you were being like a father to him."

Boomer looked at her with the cunningness of a fox and said, "I was." He then picked up a piece of steak, chewing as he waved her out of his apartment. He was starting to speak when he began to hold his chest. He struggled to say, "Call 911!"

Sheniece walked over to him and, with same coldness that he displayed, she said, "You molested my son and then blame me for it, and now you want me to save your life. What about Sayso? Who was there for him when you were molesting his little body? Your life for my son's life." She then takes his only phone from his table, where he could possibly reach it. She places it in his bedroom, on his bed and then pulls the the phone cord from the wall jack. This was to be symbolic of her revenge on Boomer. He would be unable to enter the room where he destroyed a life in order to save his own. She shut the door and left.

She returned to her apartment, plopped down on her couch and struggled to catch her breath. Tears begin to roll down her face. Two hours went by before she called 911 to report that she heard a large thump in Boomer's apartment.

Five minutes later she heard sirens and the sound of feet running up the steps. A few minutes later she looked out her window and saw the coroner's car. She knew then that Boomer was dead. But his death brought her no relief from the pain and anger she felt.

Her front door opened. It is Sayso. Sheniece gave him a blank stare.

He noticed her strange expression and questioned her about her mood. "What's wrong with you?"

Her fury prevented her from thinking before she responded. "Sayso, why didn't you tell me?"

"Tell you what?"

"That Boomer was molesting you!" she said forcefully.

Sayso almost fell off his feet, devastated that his darkest secret had been exposed. He regained his composure, then went on the defense. "Ain't nobody molested me. You're tripping, Ma," looking away in an attempt to reduce his embarrassment.

She said, "Stop, Sayso! Boomer told me himself."

Sayso continued to deny the truth until he caught the sincerity in his mother's face and, with tears in his eyes, he admitted to the molestation. "You made me trust him. I tried to tell you with my eyes, but you never looked into my eyes." He paused. "If only you had looked into my eyes."

Sheniece was devastated by her son's pain and her guilt. She walked over to him and apologized with everything in her. "Baby, I am so sorry and I wish that I could take away your hurt."

He hugged his mother, acknowledging her love for him. "I know that you are, but the memories follow me everywhere I go." Sayso dropped his head, then left the room.

Sheniece was left alone with the hate she had for a dead man, the guilt of her own negligence, and the pain carried by the most important person in her life.

Chapter Five
Rode

Sayso was now eighteen years old and had become a main player in the streets. He was known as a big time drug dealer. He drove a luxury car and always had money, which kept the girls chasing after him. He was seen as "the man" by many of the young boys in the hood. It was not so much for the things that he had, but for the compassion that he showed them. Sayso took out the time to talk to them, play basketball with them and even read to the younger kids.

Sheniece was aware of the lifestyle that he lived, but because of her guilt she was unable to chastise him.

Sayso associated with many females, but spent most of his time with a sixteen-year-old girl named Shala. The thing that made her special to him is that they had shared similar experiences. She was raised by a single mother. She had no contact with her grandmother and she, too, was molested as a young child.

But, it was the similarities which would interrupt their ability to have a solid and functional relationship. Both of them were untrusting of adults, angry at themselves and searching for their place in the world.

He continued to have a good relationship with DaQuan, who was now thirteen years old. He admired Sayso and would always tell his friends that he was Sayso's rode.

On one particular day, Sayso was home relaxing when DaQuan showed up at his door in tears.

"What up, man?" Sayso asked.

"Nothing," the little boy said.

"Come on, man, this is your rode," Sayso reminded him.

"Okay, I'll tell you. Some boys at my school were teasing me because of my sneakers. They said that I got them from Wal-Mart," DaQuan explained. He then burst out with frustration. "I told my mom not to get me these shoes!"

Sayso understood what DaQuan was going through and tried to teach him what really mattered in life. "Look, boy, you get good grades in school and you have a mother who loves you. Forget about those knuckleheads! They're just jealous," Sayso said, as he pulled out a bundle of bills. "Here, man," handing him two hundred dollars. "Go get you some new sneaks. and I'm not giving this to you because of those clowns. I'm giving it to you because you get good grades in school," Sayso assured DaQuan.

"DaQuan!"

"It's my ma." DaQuan hugged Sayso before leaving.

"DaQuan!" his mother, Miss Diss, called out again.

"I'm coming!" he called out as he tried to hide the money he had. DaQuan knew that his mother did not approve of Sayso's lifestyle or the way he earned his money.

Miss Diss noticed the bulge in DaQuan's pocket. "What's in your pocket?" she asked.

"Nothing," he said.

Realizing that he was hiding something, she pulls the money from his pocket. "Where did you get this money from?" she asked with the intensity of an Army sergeant.

"I got it from Sayso! He gave it to me so that I could buy some new sneakers. The kids in my class were teasing me about the ones that I have," DaQuan tried to explain to her.

"You listen to me and you listen good. I work hard so that you can get what you need and you don't need money from a thug," she clearly pointed out. Determined not to see her son seduced by the streets. She grabs the money.

"Sayso was only trying to help!" DaQuan squealed, attempting to defend his friend's honor.

Not moved by the plea, Miss Diss decreed that it was a trap. "It's a trap, son. It's a trap, but you will not be spun." She grabbed his hand. "Come on. You're going to give this money back." She marched him down to Sheniece's apartment. She knocks on the door.

Sayso answered. "What's up?" he asked, not ever suspecting that this encounter would forever change his life, also the fact that Miss Diss had never spoken to him or his mother in the past.

Ms Diss speaks out. "This is my son, and he does not need anything from you. If I can't get it for him, then he does not need it." She paused her ranting and, with every intention of hurting him, she said, "You may have been bought by that Boomer man, but you will not buy my son."

Sayso stood motionless like that of a wounded animal. He reaches into his pocket.

Sheniece, who was standing in the background, screamed out, "Sayso don't! Its not worth it."

"But my son is," Miss Diss said as she grabbed DaQuan's hand, then storms off.

Sayso moved slowly as he walked back into his apartment. Sheniece was speechless and unsure of what to say. He looked up at her. His eyes were welled up with tears.

He then said, with the most serious facial expression, "You see what you allowed to happen to my life?" He fell to the floor, disarming his hardcore demeanor, then began sobbing like a child. "All you had to do is open your mouth and say, 'No! You can't watch my child!' It would have stopped!" he cried.

Sheniece yearned for his pain to be transferred to her. "Oh, baby, I'm so, so sorry." She walked over to him, took his hand and began explaining why she had not spoken up. "I was raised believing that I didn't have a voice or opinion. Whenever I questioned my mother about the decisions she made, she would always respond by saying it's because I say so."

He yanked his hand from hers, then looked at hers with shear amazement before asking, "You named me with the words that robbed you of your spirit?"

"Please don't be angry!" she pleaded. "I just wanted to always be reminded of how not to treat my own child."

Sayso was unmoved by her explanation. He left the living room, returning with a suitcase.

Sheniece could not believe her eyes. She attempted to stand up, but her legs were weak and wobbling. She became absorbed by remorse. "Where are you going?" She trembles at the thought of her only child leaving her.

"I have got to get out of here, this apartment, this building, this community and this city."

Sheniece, desperate for her son to stay, said, "I know that you blame me for your pain and I am the blame. But, baby, that's why I refused to get Boomer help when I saw him having a heart attack. I just let him die!"

Sayso dropped his suitcase. He turned her way, then with extreme shock, he said, "And you thought that my pain would die with him? There is never a day that goes by that I do not see his face in front of me. I can still smell his foul odor and feel the weight of his large body on my chest. I can remember the fear, wondering when my mother would come rescue me. You see momma, I had planned on taking my dignity back by taking him to court and exposing him in front of everybody. But you took that chance away from me. Boomer died without experiencing the type of humiliation that he caused me. He got the easy way out." He then walks out the door, never looking back.

DISGUISED ARROGANCE

Sheniece felt as if her heart had been ripped from her body. She was left weak, limp and without the ability to go after her only child.

Chapter Six
Inherited Damnation

Sayso had been gone for five years. Sheniece had gotten a job working in a daycare with abused children. DaQuan had never forgotten how his mother treated his mentor. He blamed her for him leaving the city.

Miss Diss received a call from DaQuan's school, informing her of his delinquency from school. She confronted him when he got home. "DaQuan! I know that you have not been going to school and I'm not having it."

He responded with little regard for her warning. "What are you going to do? Talk bad about me like you did Sayso?"

Miss Diss tried to reason with him. "Son, I know that you are still angry about that boy leaving, but he was a bad influence on you."

DaQuan became more angry. "You judged him without knowing him! He was my friend and you chased him away, just because of what you heard."

Miss Diss realized for the first time what Sayso meant to her son. "Baby, I was trying to keep you from doing the very things that you are doing."

DISGUISED ARROGANCE

DaQuan screamed, "Did you stop me? Did you, Ma?" He then left the apartment, shutting the door behind him.

Miss Diss was left alone to hear the echoes of her son's anger.

DaQuan ran into some friends in the neighborhood. "What up?" the young men greeted each other.

Shoplift, known for his robbing, said, "Nothing much, but I can make something happen. Are ya'll in?" he asked.

DaQuan, still steaming over his fight with his mother, did not think before he answered. "I'm in."

Shoplift then disclosed his plan to rob an elderly woman. He told the group that the woman lived alone and had a lot of money. He guaranteed that the woman would be an easy target and promised that no one would get hurt.

With their limited thought out plan, they proceeded to accomplish their goal. They broke into her back door. Once in, they began looking through the drawers in the woman's kitchen. Shoplift began grabbing electronics and bragging about the money he would get when he sold them.

What they did not realize, is that the elderly woman had awakened to the commotion and had already called 911. Not knowing this, they went upstairs and, to their surprise, she was sitting up in bed. She began screaming. Shoplift began punching her about her head and telling her to shut up.

DaQuan is shocked by what he is observing. He yelled out, "Nobody was supposed to get hurt!" Then he grabs Shoplift.

"But she saw us and I ain't trying to go to jail."

They heard the police sirens and all run out of the house, going in different directions.

DaQuan ran as fast as he could, not believing what had just happened. His heart was beating so fast and pounding so loud that he did not realize that the police were running behind him. They caught him, threw him to the ground and handcuffed him.

"What are you doing? I didn't do anything!"

The police took him back to the scene where they were

holding the others. The victim was nearby, being comforted by another officer. She is asked if DaQuan was one of the intruders. The woman, remembering how DaQuan stopped her from being killed, said that she did not know.

It was possible that DaQuan would be let go until Shoplift yelled out, "He was with us! Look in his pocket," he demanded. They found the woman's jewelry.

He could not believe that his homeboy had sold him out. He was put into the police car and taken to jail. He was fingerprinted, photographed and placed in a holding cell overnight.

A few days later he saw a judge and was given a trial date. DaQuan was found guilty and convicted for assault and burglary. He was taken to another location. His cell mate was returning from work duty.

DaQuan refused to go quietly. "I ain't doing no time," he declares.

His cell mate was irritated by what he was hearing. "Oh shut up!" he demanded. "You did the crime, you do the time," lying on his bunk, "and I ain't going to listen to you for the next five years. You see, I got a lot of time so, the only thing that I have to lose is my teeth. So do not make me mad."

DaQuan, realizing that he was in the company of a real criminal, decides to become more humble. "Listen, man," he said, "I ain't trying to disrespect you, but I'm scared."

Not moved by DaQuan's admission, Dock asked, "Were you scared when you were out there hustling and robbing people?"

DaQuan put his head down, knowing that he couldn't answer the question truthfully.

Dock answered for him. "No. You were like the rest of us. All pumped up, as if bullets couldn't pierce our flesh. Not caring about anything or anybody. So stop your crying because you get no pity here."

DaQuan remembered the love of his mother and revealed his revelation to Dock. "You're wrong. My mom's got my back. She would never leave me in here!"

Dock responded with a smirk on his face. "Boy, she's at home having a party."

DaQuan was annoyed that Dock acted as if he knew the relationship that he had with his mother. He jumped up, blasting the bearer of those words. "You don't know how much my mother loves me and she ain't at home celebrating me being locked up. Man, you're tripping!"

Dock jumps down from his bunk and gets in DaQuan's face. "Na. man, you're tripping! You see, she don't have to hold her heart every time she hears bullets ringing in the streets, and she don't have to be afraid of hearing the news report. Afraid that they will be reporting that your corpse was found. Believe me, she's rejoicing. Because at least she knows where your sorry butt is."

DaQuan sat silently for a second; then, as a soldier engaged in war, rethinks his next move in this verbal war. "Man I ain't trying to hear you buzzing all in my ears," standing, "I got some peeps. Believe that!" he said.

Dock was still determined to force DaQuan to accept his fate. "Oh, you think that your baby's momma got your back? That's exactly what I'm talking about."

DaQuan admits his confidence in that very statement.

Dock hits him again with life's reality as he saw it. "Just stupid. How old is she? Fifteen? Boy, little Laquita is infatuated with you. So, for about the first, two or three years she'll come to see you, put money on your books and maybe send you a care package. But after awhile, that's going to get old. She won't like worrying about a man who can't take care of her. There won't be the drug money for diapers, or to get her nails done. The visits are going to get shorter, your books will be empty and then bam! you'll get a 'Dear John' letter, telling you how she had moved on with her life. Man, she will either hook up with another self-proclaimed baler like you, or she'll get herself together by getting hooked up with one of those government self-help programs."

Appearing to be bothered by what he had heard, DaQuan blurted, "You think you know it all!" he said with a tone of defeat.

Dock was angered by his cell mate's apparent naivety and admitted with extreme emotion. "Fool! I'm living it. I've been here for thirty years and all I've gotten is three visits, two letters and ten dollars, and I'm mad about that! But what right do I have to be mad? I made all the people I loved and loved me experience a living hell." Dock stops to catch his breath before proceeding. "Boy, ninety percent of the men in here is living it. So, welcome into our world. You are us and we are you." He then lies back down on his bunk, exhausted by his transparency.

DaQuan responds with a cool disposition. "That's all good, man, but my homeboy got my back. All I need to do is call his mother to get his cell number," although in truth, Sheniece did not know Sayso's whereabouts.

"Yea, right," Dock mumbled, not giving thought to his young cell mate's ranting.

Realizing that he had not been taken seriously, he began boasting about his friend. "That's right, my boy got clothes, cars and mad loot." He then demanded to make a call expecting to prove that he was telling the truth. "Guard! I get to make a phone call."

Dock intentionally provokes DaQuan. "Oh, you think that your Mr. Success will come here, lay out his dirty money for you and risk his own freedom?"

"Yep," said DaQuan.

"Boy, you're dumber than I thought. Did your homeboy tell you what the cost would be for lying, stealing and robbing? Huh? Did he tell you that he could never look forward because he had to always look at what was behind him? What kind of life do you have when you can't look forward to what is ahead?"

DaQuan answered the way a typical teenager would, when he/she was unable to answer to logic. "I ain't hearing you, man." He was aware that he had struck a deep wound in Dock when he suddenly thrust upon him like a hurricane appearing out of nowhere.

With tears swelling up, he grabbed DaQuan's neck. "That's what my boy said when I tried to stop him from living the life that I did," Dock struggled to say. "I did not want him to be like me. I wanted him to be somebody. Somebody that I could be proud of. I wanted to say that's my boy, loosening his grip from DaQuan's neck, hard working, respectful and decent. But he wouldn't listen. He just wouldn't listen." Walking to the opposite side of the cell. "I became so angry, and before I knew it, I hit him. The rage of my disappointment took over me. He fell. I said, 'Get up, boy!' But he didn't move. I said again. 'Get up, boy! I'm not playing with you.' His body never moved. I said, 'Get up, son! I'm not joking.' I ran over to him. He was not breathing," demonstrating his actions. "I shook him and shook him. I said, 'Come on, son. Please!' I started to breathe in him all the life I had. 'Don't you die on me! Don't you dare die on me, when all I was trying to do was save you!'" Dock was consumed with grief. He looked up with an expression of deep sorrow and admitted, "I loved my son to death."

DaQuan felt empathy for his seasoned cell mate and attempted to help him up.

Dock pushed him away. "Get off me! I don't need your pity."

DaQuan now knew that he was in a cell with a man who was angry at boys like him. "Guard!" he called out. "Man, I want to make my call. All I have to do is call my boy Sayso. He'll get me out this hell hole."

Dock, who had regained his composure, began to laugh hysterically. "Did you say Sayso?" he asked, still laughing. "You mean Sayso said so Sayso? The one who is afraid to take showers."

DaQuan was confused by Dock's behavior and even more shocked that Dock knew his mentor. "Why are you tripping?" He asked the laughing man.

Dock stopped laughing. "Call him," he said.

"What do you mean?" DaQuan replied.

Dock sits slowly back in his chair and proudly says, "Call him. He's here and he has life just like me."

DaQuan was both angered and saddened by the thought of Sayso being locked up. For, if this was true, there wouldn't be much hope for his own situation. "Guard! Guard! I want to make my phone call. I need to call my boy Sayso."

The guard approaches the cell. "Man, you need to shut up all of that noise. You're not in the streets anymore and, anyhow, Sayso won't be receiving any calls. He committed suicide in his cell last night." The guard handed DaQuan a note. "Here, man. He left this note for all of you inmates," the guard said before leaving.

DaQuan struggled to catch his breath. He dropped to the floor, feeling as if he had been hit with a ton of bricks, dropping the note.

Dock picks up the letter and begins reading it

To all who remains left behind,

I have left this world the way I lived my life; struggling, lonely and choking on my own stuff. I have never gained anything through the efforts of genuine hard work. Everything I owned was obtained by robbing, lying and inflicting fear in my peers and community. And all the time crying my own silent tears. My actions became the means for ridding myself of the perpetrator who stole my innocence. But the foul stench of this thief's existence had made its way through my bloodstream and will forever linger on. Who was I? I never knew and you will never know. I am gone now, but I leave you with these words. A life without purpose is like the remnants of running water going down the drain. Therefore, do not allow the desires of another man's heart represent the fire that ignites the passion for your own life.

Live and don't die,
Sayso

DaQuan was horrified. He screamed out for Sayso, praying that he would answer his call. He grabbed the letter from Dock and crumbled it. His sorrow turned into anger toward Sayso. "I can't believe that you punked out! Man, I believed in you. I wanted to be just like you," crying. "Man, why you go out like that? I trusted you with my life!"

Tears flow down Dock's face. He was remorseful over his treatment of DaQuan. He went to him, hugged him and said, "Man, bring meaning to your friend's life by not traveling on the same path. Get out of here and make your own footprints."

Hours had gone by since Sayso's suicide. DaQuan had remained silent the entire time. Dock decided not to impose on his mourning. The silence in the cell reeked of sadness and pain.

It was interrupted when the guard called for DaQuan. "Come on, man. You have a visitor," he said. He handcuffed him before leading him down the corridor and into the family visiting room.

DaQuan is surprised to see Sheniece. He plopped down, never looking at her.

It was apparent that Sheniece was in distress over her son's death. She took his hand, held up his chin, and with tears in her eyes, she said, "Let me look into your eyes." He turned his face away from her. "I need to look into your eyes," she pleaded. She then turned to the guard standing in the room. "Please take these handcuffs off him."

The guard informs her that they are for her protection. She looked him in the face and asked, "Does it look like I'm afraid of him?"

Frustrated by her demand, the guard asked, "Why?"

Sheniece slowly stood to her feet, staring him in his eyes and, with the confidence of a woman who knows where she had been and knows where she is going, says, "Because I say so."

Chapter Seven
Bewildered

Sheniece had returned home to the echo of her pain. She crouched on her couch, still stunned by her son's death and the manner in which he died. She looked around the apartment, the place she once considered to be her palace. Her eyes meet with a picture of Sayso as a happy smiling baby. Next to that picture, she glanced at the sad eyes of her seven year old child. *If only I had looked into his eyes.*

"I hate you, Boomer!" she screamed. "I hate you for what you did to my son! Sayso! Sayso!" she wailed, praying that he would walk through the door. "Oh, my son."

Her mourning was interrupted by a knock at her door. She ran to answer, hoping that she had been awakening from a dream and that her son would be standing on the other side of the door. To her shock, it was Marisa, her mother. Sheniece was so stunned that she was unable to speak or move.

Realizing that her daughter was genuinely shocked by her presence, Marisa spoke first. "Hello Sheniece. I just wanted to be there for you and to help you pay for Sayso's funeral arrangements."

Sheniece's heart began pounding so fast that its vibration was felt through her clothes. She was barely able to breathe. She ran to her kitchen to get a glass of water. She regained her composure, returned to her living room, where Marisa had invited herself in. Sheniece's insides burn with hatred at the sight of the woman who had rejected her, standing in her home. "You come here and dare to say you want to help me with Sayso's funeral?"

"I know there is no excuse for my absence and selfishness. I was wrong. I admit." These were words that Marisa had never uttered. "But when I heard that my only grandchild had hung himself, I became angry at myself. Sheniece, I know that I missed the chance to be there for him, but please let me be here for you."

Sheniece looked at her son's sad picture and was again reminded of the pain he had suffered. She turned to her mother in a very slow motion that appeared to give her rage momentum, screaming out from the depth of her soul, "Be here for us! I asked you to watch him for just one night and you wouldn't do that. Not even for a grandchild that you had never laid your eyes on. Do you know what happened to my son because I had no babysitter? Some man molested him and continued to abuse him for years. My baby suffered every day because of it and you wonder why he hung himself." Sheniece weakened and fell to the floor.

Marisa went over to console her.

Sheniece pushed her away and, with great contempt, she said, "You get out of my house and don't you ever come back here! Because of you, my son is dead."

Marisa stumbled backward. She stood up and started to leave, but then she stopped, and with tears streaming down her face, she said, "Sheniece, I know that I didn't do my part for you or my grandson and, believe it or not, my heart aches over it. I robbed myself of a family. But, baby, we both had a part in the neglect of Sayso. I never looked after him and you left him alone." She then crouched on the floor next to Sheniece, taking her in her arms and for the first time in twenty-two years, Marisa hugged her daughter.

Sayso would never know that his death would induce the healing of two women, bewildered by the circumstances of their yesterdays. Marisa and Sheniece had begun to talk for the first time in years and for the first time in her life since the age of ten, Sheniece felt the love of her mother.

Marisa felt comfortable enough to talk about Sayso's father. Sheniece exposed in detail the history of their relationship. Marisa empathizes with her daughter's bitterness, but told her that the man had a right to know that his son died. He would have to live with the fact that he had abandoned a young girl who was pregnant and too scared to tell him. She went on to commend Sheniece on not becoming bitter and blaming her child as she had.

Sheniece took her mother's advice and located Sayso's father. She called his home. A little boy answered. "Can I speak to Derick please?"

The boy told her to hold on. "Daddy! Some lady wants you on the phone."

Sheniece became instantly on the defense. *I dare that he would go on to have another son when her son was lying in the morgue.*

"Hello," he said, as if he didn't have a care in the world.

"Hello," she said, attempting to camouflage her true anger. "This is Sheniece. Do you remember me?"

Surprised by the phone call, he said, "Of course. How have you been?" curious to why she was calling.

Sheniece refused to have small talk. She cut straight through the charade. "Well, I'm actually at the lowest point in my life. Why is that? I have to tell you something that I should have told you a long time ago."

Interrupting her, he arrogantly says, "What?"

"You have a child by me." She could hardly contain herself.

"As a matter of fact, I do. I heard that you were pregnant and wondered if it was mine," he admits. "But the night that I saw you in the club you didn't say anything about having a child."

Infuriated by his boldness, she said, "You were with your wife!" she reminded him. "What was I supposed to say? Congratulations, I have your son."

"Well, why are you calling me after all these years?" Derick asked. "I would have given your, I mean our son child support. He would be an adult now."

"I'm only calling to inform you that my child and your son is dead," she explained.

"What?" Derick responded. "You call me after all these years to tell me that I have a dead son! He calmed down, then asked, "What was my son's name?"

"His name was Sayso," Sheniece said, as her voice quivered with emotions.

"Sayso? was he the man that hung himself in jail?"

"He was," she said as her quivers became a full expression of her mourning for her son.

Derick dropped his phone. Sheniece could hear him vomiting in the background. His son could be heard asking him if he was alright, then crying himself.

Sheniece hangs up her phone. Could it be possible that a man could truly grieve over a child that he never met? Was he feeling like Marisa? She would never know Sayso and neither would he. They get no second chance with him.

The funeral took place. It was attended by many young people. Sheniece did not know that her son had so many friends. She looked up and saw the love of her life in attendance with his wife and son.

DaQuan's mother, Miss Diss, walked up to Sheniece. "Honey, you will never know how sorry I am for what I said to your son. I was just trying to protect my son from the streets, but still they captured him."

DISGUISED ARROGANCE

Sheniece was unable to speak. But she respects the concern that this woman had for her child and with that, she hugged the remorseful mother.

She tried to drown out the cries of all the young girls. But one girl in particular had filled the room with her groans. She felt compelled to console the girl. Forgetting about her own grief, she walks over to the girl and hugs her.

The girl said, "My name is Shala and I had a baby by your son."

Sheniece was astounded by this news and, for a moment, she recovered from her tragic loss. "Why didn't you tell me or bring him over to my house?"

The girl just shrugged her shoulders and promised to take him to visit his grandmother soon.

Sheniece was ecstatic about having apart of her son remaining, She got up to give her son's eulogy…

Sayso's euology:

> No mother wants to see their child lying in a permanent state of stillness, knowing that there is nothing humanly possible to bring him back. But, my son was dead before he died. For a foul, immoral man stole his life when he was just a boy, and I was too blinded by my own stuff to see his suffering. If only I had looked into his eyes I could have stopped his pain from the malignancy of an emotional tumor which suffocated his dreams, hopes and thrill for living a successful life. Mothers, watch over your children so that one man's arrogance doesn't become your child's demise.

Chapter Eight
Freedom Rings

Miss Diss is at the prison to greet DaQuan upon his release. His incarceration had taken a toll on her health. DaQuan was taken back by his mother's gaunt look. As the gate is opened he runs to embrace her, pretending not to notice her ill appearance.

"Oh, you look good, son. I was afraid that you wouldn't look the same."

"Well, you know, I worked out every day. I didn't have anything else to do."

I'm just so glad to have you home," she admitted, as she hugs him with the little strength she had left. Miss Diss didn't waste any time finding out what he was going to do in order to stay out of trouble. "So what's your plans for the future, son?"

Joking, "Well, first a brother needs a piece of chicken, a hot shower without having ten other bodies being in the bathroom and a good night's sleep in his own bed."

"I see that prison has made you appreciate a sister, huh!" His mother says in a loving manner.

DaQuan knew what she was saying, and without uttering a word, he hugged his mother and kissed her on the forehead.

DISGUISED ARROGANCE

They arrived back in the hood. He began reliving the night he was picked up. He paused before going inside the building, knowing that he would have to pass by Sayso's old apartment, the one he admired most. The one he thought had everything. The one who killed himself because he had nothing. He braced himself for the emotions that would surface once he opened the door. It looked and smelled the same. He felt the large discomfort of a lump being formed in his throat. He was careful not to wear his uneasiness on his face. He did not want to concern his mother. He opened the door to his apartment and was immediately greeted by the comfort of it's environment.

He stood glancing from the outside, marveling at it's cleanliness, sweet aroma and comfort of a loving home.

His mother became inpatient with his idleness. "Boy! You don't have to wait for someone to give you permission. Walk on to the other side." Then, laughing, she said, "You be free, boy, you be free." She nudges him into the apartment.

DaQuan laughed so hard that the pain of the past was lifted from his heart.

Miss Diss treated DaQuan to the things that he desired. He took a long hot shower, he devoured some home fried chicken and had a nice warm bed waiting for him.

DaQuan immediately falls asleep in his nice warm bed after eating.

His mother was thrilled to have her son home and was thankful to see him resting peacefully. She was, however, concerned for his well being now that he was back. She didn't want him to end up back in jail.

The evening had gone and the sun had risen.

"DaQuan!" his mother called out, as she had prepared a breakfast fit for a king. There were home fries, sausage, grits, eggs, honey biscuits and fresh orange juice.

Forgetting that he was no longer incarcerated, DaQuan called out his prison number. "…5673212 here."

Miss Diss felt for what her son had experienced. She whispered, "You're home, baby, you're home."

Embarrassed by his display, he walked past his mom and goes into the bedroom. He washed, got dressed and ate before going out to check out the hood.

The boarded up buildings had increased. He wondered if he would be able to find a job. As he continued walking, he passed a billboard with the pictures of three of his dead friends. He wondered if being incarcerated actually saved his life. What had the world come to, when being behind bars was a better option than being free. He wanted to be free. But, how was he going to start fresh? There were no jobs, especially for a felon like him. The one thing that he did know was that he would not disappoint his mother again.

He went back home to find his mother lying on the floor. He was devastated. He ran over to her. Her hands were cold and clammy.

She opened her eyes, then closed them again. He called 911.

The paramedics arrived and Miss Diss was transported to the hospital.

DaQuan could not believe was was happening as he sat in the emergency waiting room. Tears begin to well up. He felt guilty for how he had treated his mother in the past, when all she wanted was to keep him out of trouble. He experienced a feeling of loneliness and emptiness. He missed the security of the prison. At least he knew where he would eat and sleep.

His thoughts were interrupted by a tap on his shoulder. The nurse instructs him to follow her.

His heart jumped for joy when he saw his mother smiling and sitting up. "Mom, you scared me! I am so glad to see you smiling."

The doctor stepped in the room and explained to him that his mother was a diabetic and became sick when her sugar level had gone up.

This news was shocking to him. He had no idea that his mother was sick. She had been diagnosed while he was in prison. He looked at his mother, trying not to show his anger with her. "Mom, you never said anything about being sick in any of the letters you sent me."

"What difference would have telling you made?" she answered for him. "Nothing."

He knew that she was right, so he ended the conversation.

The doctor released her with her discharge instructions.

This experience had motivated DaQuan to beat the odds against him. He did not want his mother to end up on her death bed without her having any good memories of him as an adult. He would not let the evidence of the streets prevent him from seeing beyond them. He would not allow the arrogance of his environment to victimize him, as it had done his mentor, Sayso. He would not let his past dictate his future. He would learn from the sting of its consequences. He would indeed be free.

Chapter Nine
Old Acquaintances, New Choices

DaQuan sat in front of his apartment building as he pondered his plan for success. Shala, Sayso's girlfriend came walking by. She was holding a little boy's hand. He had heard that she was pregnant by Sayso. The closer she got, he knew that it was true. The little boy looked just like Sayso. But Shala looked terrible. She was thin and unkempt.

"Hey, what's up, girl?" he ask. "Is that little Sayso?" thrilled that a part of his friend would still live on.

"He looks like him," she answered, with the tone of a scorned woman. "When you get out, boy?" she asked, not waiting for him to answer her first question.

"Two weeks ago, baby girl," he said with the pride of a peacock strutting its feathers.

Eager to deflate his ego, she asked, "For how long? You know whenever one of you knuckleheads get out, you go right back in for doing the same ole dumb thing."

Not understanding her obvious bitterness, he snapped back at her. "There you go, putting a brother down before he gets started." He decided to address her anger. "Why are you so angry? I know that you miss Sayso and all that, but, girl, you're tripping."

Looking at his naivety, with tears in her eyes, she asked, "You didn't hear?"

"Hear what?" he asked.

Then, with the roar of a wounded lion, she blurted out, "He gave me AIDS! Then he had the nerve to kill himself, leaving me to live with this disease."

Not expecting to hear that disclosure, he stands up and in the defense of his friend, denied her statement. "Shala, you don't know where you got burned. You slept around with everybody."

She pushed DaQuan. "Why do you think he killed himself?"

"It wasn't because of that," he assures her. "Shala you better go find the thug that burned you," refusing to believe what she is saying.

"Why would I lie on a dead man? He knew he had it and didn't care about me or his baby. He took the easy way out."

DaQuan, still refusing to hear her, "At least your alive," he said with a foolish heart.

"Alive!" she proclaimed. "What man will want me?"

"If you get off that crack, maybe you can get a man. Now get away from my building."

She left, not saying another word, knowing it was useless to try. She took her son's hand and left.

He sat attempting to block out what had just occurred, when he saw his closest classmate, Darius.

Darius was one of the smartest boys in the school. He would always receive awards for having achieved academic excellence. He was also a great athlete and led the school's football team to many championships. He was the only one who never smoked, drank, took drugs or used the girls. So how was it that he was moving around in a wheelchair? DaQuan took a second look to make sure he was seeing correctly. It was Darius. Darius was really in a wheelchair.

Darius rolled up to DaQuan. "What's up man? Its good to see you, DaQuan."

DaQuan was surprised by his friend's good spirit. "It's good to see you too," he replied.

Darius observed the shock on DaQuan's face, and said out loud what his classmate was thinking. "Before you ask, man, let me tell you. I was dating this woman who was separated from her husband. He found us together at her house and shot me twelve times."

DaQuan was stunned. "Man you waited until you got to be a grown man to get sprung over a woman," he said.

Darius assured DaQuan that he was still blessed. He had married that woman, they had two beautiful children and was employed as a computer engineer. He went on to say that his life had been changed and that he was a minister in his church.

Darius invited DaQuan over to his home and to his church. Then a van pulls up and the most beautiful woman that he had ever seen steps out. She walks over to Darius, kisses him and then assisted him with getting into the van. Sitting in the back were two children, greeting him with great excitement.

DaQuan realized that, although paralyzed, Darius's life was much fuller than his. He was hit with the reality that one's handicap, whether physical, emotional or social did not mean that their ability to live was at a permanent loss. He concluded that as long as one continued to inhale the air they breathe as the fuel to go on, they could proclaim success for their future. He would see the inhalation of God's air as a privilege, not to be taken for granted. DaQuan had become more inspired by his future than his past. He had visualized his future. He did not know how his success would come, but he was confident that it would happen.

He went into his apartment. His mother noticed a difference in his face.

"Your face is glowing, honey. Did you get a job?" she asked.

"Not yet. I just ran into somebody who really let me know that I could make it."

DISGUISED ARROGANCE

Miss Diss walked over to her son, stared him in his eyes and decreed, "I see greatness in your eyes."

He had done it. He had brought a gleam to his mother's face. She was proud of him. He recognized that for that second, the mistakes of his past had been erased from her mind.

Determined to keep that look on his mother's face, he went in his room to look through the classifieds. He was on a mission to change the course of his life. He would no longer walk in the footsteps of another man's lead. He would make his own footprints. However, he had dropped out of the eleventh grade and could not find any job that he was qualified to do. Where would he find someone who would hire a felon, who was street savvy, with little education.

He went out every day looking for a job. He was told that they were not hiring, or told to come back later. Later never came. DaQuan had begun to get discouraged. He started drinking behind his mother's back.

One day while drinking in the park, he met up with "Juice," the brother of "Shoplift." He was given that name because he was always looking for juice to put in his alcohol.

"What's cracking, man?"

"I'm just chilling," DaQuan said, hoping to end the conversation.

But Juice made himself comfortable on the bench next to DaQuan. "Well, what you been doing with yourself?" Juice asked, with his words all slurred, apparently, already intoxicated.

"I'm just trying to find a J.O.B."

Juice pulled out a small bag of crack cocaine and invited DaQuan to smoke it with him.

DaQuan declined the offer. "Man, I'm trying to stay clean and get my life together."

Juice felt shrunken by the rejection. He changes the conversation. "My boy got a good job and I can hook you up with him."

"Man, you know that I am a felon, DaQuan admitted reluctantly.

"So is he, a felon times two."

DaQuan felt a glitter of hope. "Well, hook a brother up."

"I will, man. Give me your number and I'll have him call you tonight," Juice promised.

DaQuan felt as if he is on his way to fulfilling his destiny. He threw his beer in the trash.

Chapter Ten
Betrayal of a Perpetrator

DaQuan had just returned home from picking up a newspaper. He prepared to settle in before reading the local news and searching the classifieds. He would always read the local news headlines first. That was the way he could keep up with what was happening in the hood.

The headlines read:

> Boomer, a known pedophile had molested several boys and infected them with the HIV virus. Ten of them have come forward and one of them committed suicide after learning that he had developed full blown AIDS. This man was never brought to justice because he died of a heart attack several years ago.

Daquan's breath was almost taken away. Shala was telling the truth! He balled up the paper and then let out a screeching sound.

"What's wrong?" his mother asked as she entered his room. He didn't answer.

She picked up the crumbled paper and read the headline. "Oh, DaQuan, I am so sorry." She grabbed her son and held him as tight as she could. "Listen, baby, even in his death Boomer will pay for what he did. You see, anyone that thought good of him will know the truth about him. But, most importantly, when this world is over, he will surely answer for his crimes. Not even in death can a murderer escape his judgment."

DaQuan didn't respond to his mother's revelation. He headed for the door But, before leaving, he ask his mother for Sheniece's new address.

"Why?"

"Just tell me, where she lives!" he demanded.

"DaQuan, she lives in a house on Ship Drive."

He grabbed his coat and ran out the door.

His heart and brain collided with anger, hurt and sorrow for his friend. His anger was further fueled by the fact that Boomer was dead and could not be brutalized for what he did. He would not be able to avenge his friend's torment.

He arrived at Sheniece's house. He took a deep breath before knocking on her door, not sure of his purpose for being there. He knocked and she answered.

Surprised to see him, "Hi, DaQuan. I heard that you were out and was wondering when you would come to see me."

He stepped inside, sat down and looked down to the floor.

"Let me look into your eyes and see what's in your heart," Sheniece asked.

He looked up, then asked if she had seen the paper.

"I have it, but have not read it yet."

"Read it," he said.

She went into another room and returned with the paper. "What am I looking for?" she inquired. He directed her to look at the local news section.

Her mouth dropped, then tears begin to stream down her face. "My baby was betrayed by a pedophile! she cried out.

"Why did you trust him?" DaQuan asked.

Feeling his own pain, Sheniece was shaken by the question. "What did you say?" believing that she may have misheard him.

"Why did you leave Sayso with that man?" he repeated.

"I did not leave him with that Boomer. He went into my house and took advantage of my son when I wasn't home."

"But you left him alone! You left a little boy home by himself in an unlocked apartment." He refused to excuse her from her irresponsibility.

"Listen, DaQuan, I was young and stupid, and I really did forget to lock the door," she tried to explain.

"But you should have stayed home!" he shouted. "My mother never left me! Not once." DaQuan declared.

She felt the conviction of her actions and became overwhelmed with guilt. The tears continued streaming down her face. She looked in his eyes, and said, Well, you should be thankful for your mother. A woman who knew how to protect you. I didn't know how to protect my son and because of it, not only did this man contaminate his body and destroy his dignity, but he also stole his motivation to live. What had devastated me the most was that I aided this pedophile in taking the easy way out. I thought that I was helping my son by letting this man die before my eyes. In actuality, I failed Sayso again."

DaQuan looked at this wounded woman and developed great compassion for her. "Sheniece, you will only have failed Sayso if you don't learn from the experience. You have to use it as the flame that ignites you to overcome it," DaQuan tells her. He hugs her and for the first time since the exposure of her son's molestation, she felt love from a child who understood her pain.

Chapter Eleven
Employed with a Cost

DaQuan was home looking through the paper when the phone rang.

It was Juice's friend Monsel. "Is this DaQuan?"

"What's up?"

"I'm "Juice's friend Monsel. He told me that you were looking for a job."

"That's right, man!" DaQuan said with excitement.

"Look, man, I work at an exclusive hangout called Impressions."

"You know that I'm a felon," he said, getting that barrier out of the way.

"Man, I am a felon too. All they want you to do is come to work, look good and let the good people in and keep the bad people out." Monsel explained. "Call my boss, Mr. Vicks, and tell him that I sent you. The number is 254-555-9878."

"Thank you so much, man, and tell Juice I said thank him too." DaQuan could hardly dial the phone number fast enough. He called Mr. Vicks and was invited to come in for an interview.

DISGUISED ARROGANCE

DaQuan was mesmerized by the club. Its contemporary decor made him feel as if he had entered into Hollywood. There was plush red carpet, tables made from thick and meticulously cut glass, and elegant chandeliers hanging from the ceiling.

He was met by Mr. Vicks and taken into his office, which looked like a presidential suite. DaQuan was invited to sit down. He was asked why he wanted to work for him.

DaQuan explained to him that he wanted to change the path that his life had taken. He went on to divulge that he wanted to have a legitimate work history so that he could make his mother proud.

Mr. Vicks went on to ask him if he could trust him, being that he was a felon.

DaQuan revealed that he had lived the life of a criminal, followed in the footsteps of a criminal and had lost the real purpose in his life as a criminal. "I am now ready for a new beginning."

Mr. Vicks appeared surprised by his openness. He offered DaQuan the job and eleven dollars an hour.

DaQuan accepted without hesitation. He was so excited that he forgot to ask about any other benefits. He could hardly wait to tell his mother.

She was asleep when he arrived. He awakened her.

She looked up. "Honey, it must be important for you to wake me up."

"I got a job!" he blurted out with great excitement.

"What will you be doing?" she asked.

"I'm going to be a greeter," he reports. "You know, like a bouncer. I'll be keeping the rowdy people out."

"You be careful, son. That type of work can be dangerous," Ms Diss warned.

"You won't have to worry, Mom. It's a real nice place," as he gets ready for his first night of work.

The place looked more beautiful than it did when it was empty. The people were well dressed and the clientele consisted of rich Caucasians, African Americans, Mexican Americans, and even Asians. There were luxury cars in the parking complex. He was being exposed to a world that he could only dream of.

Jontu, the assistant to Mr. Vicks, trained DaQuan. DaQuan learned the ropes to the job very fast and he loved every moment of it. He shook the hands of wealthy men. He loved the world that he was viewing and envisioned the day when he would be one of the guests and not a greeter. He observed thousands of legal dollars being made, so he thought.

DaQuan had been employed for six months. His paychecks had become the symbol for the new direction that his life had taken. His money was legal. He purchased a used car and bought his mother her first complete living room set.

He remembered how Sayso had looked out for him and decided to do the same for his son. He bought "Lil Sayso" some clothes and takes them to Shala's house. He knocks on her apartment door. The little boy opens the door.

"Shala! Shala!" he called out, irritated that she was not up with her son.

She came stumbling into the living room. "What are you doing in my house?" She asked, as irritated as he was.

"I'm in your house because your six-year-old let me in. What's wrong with you? You know what happened to his father because his mother wasn't watching him. Do you want the same thing to happen to him?" DaQuan said, all in one reprimanding breath.

"My son knows that he is not to answer my door. Didn't I tell you never to go to the door!" she screamed at the six-year-old child.

"That's what kids do," putting the blame back on her. DaQuan said, "And look at this house! Sayso would have never allowed his son to live like this."

DISGUISED ARROGANCE

"I'm sick of hearing about Sayso," she admitted. "He is not here! I accept it and you need to accept it too."

"Oh, I accept it," DaQuan assured her. "I also accept that you are not doing right by his son."

Shala became enraged, crying out, "I can't take care of him because of all the medication that I take. It makes me weak and so sick that I can hardly get out of my bed. So what am I supposed to do? Too bad your boy is not here to help me." She then sits down, picking up her son. Appearing exhausted, she questioned his purpose for being there.

"I came to drop off some clothes for him." DaQuan put the clothes down and turned to leave. However, he paused, and with a sympathetic plead, he advised Shala to reach out to Sheniece, Sayso's mother before leaving. Drained by the interaction between Shala and himself, he went to rest before going to work.

He gets up five hours later and then prepares for work. His job was the highlight of his life. He arrived and immediately began his usual routine. He checkd the guest list, made sure that the menus were in place, then provids water, fruit and snacks to the musicians. Next he gets in place at the front door.

Three hours had gone by when he noticed that some of the guests were underage girls. One of the girls was only fourteen years of age, although she looked much older. He knew this because the girl was his friend's babysister. They had apparently gotten fake identification.

He went to inform his boss. "Mr. Vicks, some teenage girls are trying to get in," DaQuan divulged. He went on to ask if he should put them out.

"Put them out? This is the night that our money is made," Mr. Vicks explained.

"But those are high school kids," DaQuan squeals. "One of them I know is only fourteen years old."

Mr. Vicks sits back in a chair and says, "Did they have legal pictured identification stating that they are at least eighteen years of age?"

"Yes, but they're fake," DaQuan emphasized.

"That's not my concern, and don't make it yours if you want to stay employed here."

As the months went on, DaQuan continued to observe young teenagers coming to the club. He watched as they went off into private rooms. He tried to ignore it, but the convictions of his heart wouldn't allow him to.

He again approached Mr. Vicks about what he had observed, and again he was warned that his job was in jeopardy. He was told to focus on being a greeter and not on scrutinizing the guests. His boss gave him an ultimatum by saying, "If you want to keep your job, you don't see nothing, you don't hear nothing and you don't know nothing" Now go and do your job. You're good at it," Mr. Vicks said in a threatening and patronizing manner.

Chapter Twelve
Through the Eyes of a Conscience

DaQuan continued to work for Mr. Vicks, but the enthusiasm that was once there had dissipated. It had now become the drudgery in his life. He had become the spectator to the exploitation of young people and he hated it. But it was a job and how he made his legal money. It was supposed to have aided him on his journey toward his new path. He tried hard to shake his moral convictions. Doing so would have made his job bearable.

He made peace with the battle that was going on in his head by telling himself that he was on a mission to stay out of trouble. If others wanted to mess up their lives, that would be their choice. This excuse would suffice for a while, as a bandage concealing his moral turmoil.

However, this bandage was unable to contain the torment he was experiencing when he spotted Shala. She was going into one of the back rooms with one of the male patrons. He could not believe his eyes. He walked over to the two, stopping them before they got to their destination. He grabbed Shala's arm. "What are you doing here, girl?" he blurted out.

She pulled away from him. "Get your hands off of me!" she blurted out back at him. "You are not my father!" she screamed.

"You know that you shouldn't be here and I know that you don't plan to be with this man," he said, disgusted at the thought.

"DaQuan! Stay out of my business. I'm doing what I have to," she tried to explain.

Mr. Vicks noticed the commotion and went over to investigate. "What's the problem?" he asked, aware of the tension between Shala and DaQuan.

"He is all in my business, sir," Shala said, beating her adversary to the punch. She went on to say, "I paid to be here and I'm over eighteen years of age. So why am I being harassed by your worker?"

Mr. Vicks looks at DaQuan, waiting for him to give a logical explanation for his actions toward this patron. "Why are you bothering this customer?" he inquires.

DaQuan was extremely aggravated and attempted to enlighten his employer about the circumstances, without exposing her business. "She just shouldn't be here."

Mr. Vicks directed DaQuan to follow him to his office. "What is your problem, man?" Mr. Vicks asked as they entered the office.

"That girl is burned. You can't let her hang out with these men," DaQuan pleaded.

Mr. Vicks grabbed him by the throat. "Listen, punk, you don't come into my establishment and tell me how to run things." He went on to say, "You see, I don't care if she scars them for life, as long as they pay to make it happen."

Pulling away, DaQuan looked directly into the eyes of the man who was going to help change his life for the good. "Do you not understand that these men have wives and children at home?" He went on to ask, "How can you participate in the destruction of innocent people?"

Mr. Vicks sat back and, without any remorse, told DaQuan

that if he did not like the way he ran things, he could leave. He then displayed a smirk, knowing that DaQuan would have a hard time finding someone who would hire a felon.

The sly smirk enraged DaQuan. He leaned over the large desk and assured Mr. Vicks that he would panhandle in the streets before selling his soul out to the devil. The old DaQuan rose up. He grabbed Mr. Vicks by his shirt. "The next time you even think about laying your hands on me, I will bust you up and leave you to die. "He then headed for the door.

Mr. Vicks jumped up, making a threat of his own. " Don't let your words dig a grave for your corpse," he said as DaQuan waved him off.

He was angered by the arrogance of this man, so much so, that he decided to deflate his ego.

He went to the police department and disclosed the illegal activity going on at Mr. Vicks' club. He had regained his dignity, but lost his job. He would not tell his mother about him being fired and the circumstances that led to his termination.

She did, however, notice the gloom on his face. "You look like you lost your best friend. What happened to all of that excitement," she asked.

"Oh, I don't know, life has a way of taking it from you," he responded in a spirit of defeat.

"No, baby. Life can't take it away. You have to give it away by giving into the pressures of it's existence," Miss Diss said, like a woman possessing a lot of wisdom. She went on to say, "You're only defeated when you quit, but as long as you keep trying, your life remains your own guide toward your predestined destiny."

A few days later, while watching the local news, DaQuan was surprised by the headlines. Mr. Vicks had been arrested on charges of soliciting prostitution, the corruption of minors and other charges. He could not believe what he was seeing. He jumped up. He had done a good deed. He had stopped a man from ruining the lives of minors and the innocent family members of married men who would have become the victims of his immorality.

Out came Mr. Vicks and his workers in handcuffs. All of a sudden, being unemployed did not matter. He had gained something that money could not buy. He had his integrity. But a closer look reveals an image of Shala being handcuffed along with several other women. A huge feeling of guilt overshadowed his jubilance. Where was "Lil Sayso?"

DaQuan grabbed his jacket, went to the county jail and bailed her out. He used the money he had saved up for his own apartment. After about five hours of him waiting, Shala came walking down the corridor.

"What are you doing here?" she asked when she saw him sitting there, not knowing that he was the one who had bailed her out.

"I bailed you out so that you could be home with your son, that's what I'm doing here," he informed her. "Where is he, anyway?" he questioned.

"Why are you so worried about my son?" Shala asked with little appreciation for what he had done for her. She selfishly said, "I would be worried about myself if I were you. The word is that you sold out Mr. Vicks. You better watch your back because he pays people to get rid of his problems."

"I ain't worried about him," DaQuan assured her, annoyed by her ungratefulness. "I helped you out and now you're talking all of this smack! I should have left you locked up. Just go home and take care of your son," he said before walking off.

He returned home to find his mother sleeping in a chair. He wakes her up.

"Why didn't you go to bed?"

She told him that she had received a strange phone call, which made her worry about him.

"What did the caller say?" he asked. "What did the caller say, Momma?"

DISGUISED ARROGANCE

"Well, he asked me if I had life insurance for you." She slowly sat up, looked deep into his eyes and asked if everything was okay with him.

He assures her that he was not in any trouble, then helped her to bed.

He did not think about it again until he received a threat on the phone. The caller asked if he had his affairs in order. He hung up and told his mother that he received another prank call and told her to have her telephone number changed. He told her that there was nothing for her to worry about, but changing the number would stop the prank calls.

In truth, DaQuan had become concerned. He now believed that there was really a hit out on him. He decided that it would be better for him to move out of his mother's apartment. He called Sheniece to ask if he could stay with her, at least until he got on his feet.

Without hesitation, she told him that he could.

How ironic, he thought. *The woman who could not protect her own son was now providing a safe haven for him.*

He informed his mother that he would be moving out. Miss Diss was devastated. He explained to her that it was time that he stood on his own two feet. He went on to tell her that he would visit with her every day.

He packed his things and headed off to Sheniece's house. He got in his car and drove.

He noticed a black truck following him. Shots rang out. DaQuan ducked onto a side street, losing his pursuer. He made it to Sheniece's house safely.

She observed the panic in his face. "What's wrong, DaQuan?" she asked.

He did not want to alarm her, so he told her that he was just tired.

Sheniece showed him the room that she had prepared for him. She then offered him something to eat.

He could smell the aroma of his favorite food, home fried chicken. It's savory aroma penetrated his nostrils with its presence, allowing him to forget about the threat that had been made on his life. He sat down to eat what his friend had prepared for him.

He looked up and saw a picture of Sayso facing him. For the first time since hearing the words of his mentor's final words, he looked at him with the up most respect and admiration. For even out of his own pain was he trying to motivate other young people from becoming victims. The inspiration of this revelation made it easy for him to rest and he slept without any worry throughout the night. Tomorrow would be a better day

He woke in the morning ready to conquer the day. He showered, got dressed and ate breakfast. He called his mother to say good morning and to inform her that he was on his way to see her. Her phone rang, but there was no answer.

Maybe she has gone for a walk, he thought. He decided to surprise her by being there when she returned. DaQuan felt that it would be better for him to walk knowing that the people who were looking for him would recognize his car.

He arrived at his mother's apartment to find her door open and her television blaring. It was not like her to leave her door open and the volume of her television blasting in the hall. His heart began beating fast. His legs were weak as he walked in the apartment.

"Mom!" he called out, hoping that she would come out to answer his call.

The apartment was a mess, another sign that something was wrong. And then he turned to find his mother lying in a pool of blood on her kitchen floor. She had been shot in her head.

He screamed out from the depths of his soul. "Why did they come after you! You had nothing to do with them!" he cried out.

His mother was dead. He sat holding his mother's lifeless body and, at that moment, contemplated ending his own life. He had nothing to live for. He had tried to perform a courageous act, which should have changed his own legacy and because of it, his mother lied dead in his arms.

The neighbors were alerted by his scream and called 911. The ambulance, police and coroner arrived. They took her body away.

DaQuan sat on the floor for hours until coming to terms with the decision to end his life. He left to retrieve his gun from Sheniece's house. He would end his own misery. He would not let Mr. Vicks have that pleasure.

On his way to fulfill his goal, he passed by Shala's apartment building. He heard the sound of a child's unusual crying. He denied the sting of his own pain and went to investigate the origin of the child's distress. He immediately knew that the sound was coming from Shala's apartment.

He pushed the door open. It was unlocked. He found "Lil Sayso" standing over his mother's body. Next to her were empty medication bottles. Her body was cold and stiff. She was dead. He could not believe that he had been forced to face two deaths all in the same day.

He called the police, who then called the coroner. They took her body away.

The police left without asking about the little boy. They assumed that he belonged to DaQuan. He did not have the strength to tell them different.

The little boy had stopped crying and was staring up at him. He attempted to say something to soothe the child, but realized that he did not know his real name. He had always referred to him as "Lil Sayso."

"Hey, little man, what is your name?" DaQuan asked.

The little boy paused before answering, as if he knew he possessed some great secret. "My name is Promise."

DaQuan was blown away by what he had heard. But somehow the sound of his name ignited a desire in him to keep living. He grabbed some of the child's things and headed for

Sheniece's house, the woman who had compromised her own son's safety had again become the safe-haven for him, and now for her parentless grandchild.

With "Promise" in his arms, he began walking up the street when he noticed the same black truck following him. He took off running, passing by Sheniece's house. He did not want to put her in danger too.

He ran to a place known as "Homeless Blvd." It was known for it's homeless occupants. DaQuan ran between the filled boxes, trying hard not to impose on the people inside them. He looked back to see if he had lost his pursuer. In doing so, he bumped into one of the boxes. He struggled to hold onto "Promise," not wanting to drop him in the confusion. The box tipped over, exposing an entire family to the outside.

DaQuan was very apologetic. "I'm so sorry."

The man in the box looked up, and said, "Whatever you're running to, man, don't stop until you get there." He went on to say, with the most hopeless eyes that DaQuan had ever looked into, "I became overwhelmed by my circumstances, giving into the power of my temporary encounters. Man, keep running until you find the purpose that you were created for, which will be the blueprint toward embracing your destiny."

DaQuan took the advice of that homeless man. He obtained his GED certificate, went on to college to earn an undergraduate degree in child psychology and later went on to law school, where he later became a lawyer and later a judge. He specialized in cases which dealt with the prosecution of child molesters and pedophiles. Sheniece and Marisa both raised "Promise" and became the owners of a twenty-four hour daycare center named "Because We Care So"